THIS CANDLEWICK BOOK BELONGS TO:

Philip + Joseph
Fitzgerald

First U.S. paperback edition 1994
First published in Great Britain in 1992 by Walker Books Ltd., London.

Library of Congress Cataloging-in-Publication Data

Blake, Jon.
[Daley B.!]
You're a hero, Daley B.! / by Jon Blake ; illustrated by Axel Scheffler.—1st U.S. pbk. ed.
"First published in Great Britain in 1992 by Walker Books Ltd., London"—T.p. verso.
Previously published as: Daley B.!
Summary: Daley B.'s many questions about his identity and how he should live
his life are answered when Jazzy D. pays a visit to the woodlands.
ISBN 1-56402-078-9 (hardback.)—ISBN 1-56402-367-2 (pbk.)
[1. Identity—Fiction. 2. Rabbits—Fiction.] I. Scheffler, Axel, ill. II. Title.
PZ7.B554Yo   1994
[E]—dc20   93-34824

2 4 6 8 10 9 7 5 3 1

Printed in Hong Kong

The pictures in this book were done in
watercolor, crayon, and ink.

Candlewick Press
2067 Massachusetts Avenue
Cambridge, Massachusetts 02140

You're a Hero, Daley B.!

by
Jon Blake

illustrated by
Axel Scheffler

CANDLEWICK PRESS
CAMBRIDGE, MASSACHUSETTS

Daley B. didn't
know what
he was.

"Am I a monkey?" he said.
"Am I a koala?"
"Am I a porcupine?"

Daley B. didn't know where to live.

"Should I live
in a cave?"
he said.

"Should I live in a nest?"

"Should I live in a web?"

Daley B. didn't know what to eat.

"Should I
eat fish?"
he said.

"Should I eat potatoes?"

"Should I eat worms?"

Daley B. didn't know why his feet were so big.

"Are they for water-skiing?" he said.

"Are they for the mice to sit on?"

"Are they to keep the rain off?"

Daley B. saw the birds in the tree and decided he would live in a tree.

Daley B. saw the squirrels eating acorns
and decided he would eat acorns.

But he still didn't know why his feet were so big.

One day there was great panic in the woods. All the rabbits gathered beneath Daley B.'s tree. "You must come down at once, Daley B.!" they cried. "Jazzy D. is coming!" "Who is Jazzy D.?" asked Daley B. The rabbits were too excited to answer. They scattered across the grass and vanished into their burrows.

Daley B. stayed in his tree, nibbled another
acorn, and wondered about his big feet.

Jazzy D. crept out of the bushes.
Her teeth were as sharp as broken glass, and
her eyes were as quick as fleas.

Jazzy D. sneaked around the burrows, but
there was not a rabbit to be seen.

Jazzy D. looked up.
Daley B. waved.

Jazzy D. began to climb the tree.
The other rabbits poked out their
noses and trembled.

"Hello," said Daley B. to Jazzy D.

"Are you a badger?"

"Are you an elephant?"

"Are you a duck-billed platypus?"

Jazzy D. crept closer. "No, my friend," she whispered. "I am a weasel."

"Do you live in a pond?" asked Daley B.

"Do you live in a dam?"   "Do you live in a kennel?"

Jazzy D. crept closer still.
"No, my friend," she hissed,
"I live in the darkest corner of the woods."

"Do you eat cabbages?" asked Daley B.

"Do you eat insects?"

"Do you eat fruit?"

Jazzy D. crept right up to Daley B.
"No, my friend," she rasped. "I eat rabbits!
Rabbits like *you*!"

Daley B.'s face fell.
"Am I … a rabbit?" he stammered.

Jazzy D. nodded . . . and licked her lips . . .

Daley B. didn't have to think. Quick as a flash, he kicked out with his massive feet. Jazzy D. sailed through the air, far far away, back where she came from.

The other rabbits jumped and cheered
and hugged each other.
"You're a hero, Daley B.!" they cried.

"That's funny," said Daley B.
"I thought I was
a rabbit."

JON BLAKE was born in 1954. He has developed ways to use video and drama with children and has also written plays for television and the stage. He particularly enjoys writing about characters who experience some sort of danger. "Children love to see a character in danger come out all right in the end," he says, "like Daley B."

AXEL SCHEFFLER was born in Germany in 1957. He has worked as a free-lance illustrator since 1985. In creating the art for *You're a Hero, Daley B.!*, his first picture book, he especially enjoyed drawing the smaller animals, although he claims to have had a tricky time with the weasel.